A SUBJECT OF
SCANDAL AND CONCERN

A Subject of Scandal and Concern

A Play for Television
by
JOHN OSBORNE

FABER AND FABER
London

First published in 1964
by Faber and Faber Limited
This Edition published 1972
by Faber and Faber Limited
3 Queen Square, London, W.C.1
Printed in Great Britain
by Latimer Trend & Co. Ltd., Whitstable
All rights reserved

ISBN 0 571 08348 X

CHARACTERS

GEORGE HOLYOAKE

MRS. HOLYOAKE

CHAIRMAN

MAITLAND

MRS. HOLYOAKE'S SISTER

BROTHER-IN-LAW

MR. BUBB

CHAIRMAN OF THE MAGISTRATES

CAPTAIN LEFROY

MR. PINCHING

CAPTAIN MASON

MR. COOPER

MR. JONES

JAILER

CLERK TO THE ASSIZES

MR. JUSTICE ERSKINE

MR. ALEXANDER

MR. BARTRAM

CHAPLAIN

THE NARRATOR

FIRST PERFORMANCE

The first performance in Great Britain of *A Subject of Scandal and Concern* was given on BBC Television on 6th November, 1960. It was directed by Tony Richardson and the sets were designed by Tony Abbott. The cast was as follows:

GEORGE HOLYOAKE	*Richard Burton*
MRS. HOLYOAKE	*Rachel Roberts*
CHAIRMAN	*George Howe*
MAITLAND	*Colin Douglas*
MRS. HOLYOAKE'S SISTER	*Hope Jackman*
BROTHER-IN-LAW	*Hamish Roughead*
MR. BUBB	*Donald Eccles*
CHAIRMAN OF THE MAGISTRATES	*Willoughby Goddard*
CAPTAIN LEFROY	*David C. Browning*
MR. PINCHING	*John Ruddock*
CAPTAIN MASON	*Ian Ainsley*
MR. COOPER	*Robert Cawdron*
MR. JONES .	*Charles Carson*
JAILER	*John Dearth*
CLERK TO THE ASSIZES	*William Devlin*
MR. JUSTICE ERSKINE	*George Devine*
MR. ALEXANDER	*Nicholas Meredith*
MR. BARTRAM	*Nigel Davenport*
CHAPLAIN	*Andrew Keir*
THE NARRATOR	*John Freeman*

ACT ONE

*The stone corridor of a jail. A steel door opens and
there is a sound of heavy boots walking smartly.
The camera picks up the polished boots of a
policeman, the boots only. Behind, a pair of civilian
brogues come into vision. Presently both pairs stop
outside a wooden door. The door opens and we see
into a bare room, furnished only by a small wooden
table and two chairs.*

*As the camera tracks on to the table, the door is
heard to slam, a briefcase comes into vision, is
opened, and a thick typewritten manuscript is
produced. The camera holds it in closer, the title
page reads—"A Subject of Scandal and Concern".
After a few moments, it is tossed with a thump
on to the table where it lies. The camera tracks
back from it to take in the Narrator sitting on the
table.*

NARRATOR: Good evening. I am a lawyer. My name is
unimportant as I am not directly involved in
what you are about to see. What I am introducing
for you is an entertainment. There is no reason
why you should not go on with what you are
doing. What you are about to see is a straight-
forward account of an obscure event in the
history of your—well my—country. I shall simply
fill in with incidental but necessary information,
like one of your own television chairmen in fact.
You will not really be troubled with anything
unfamiliar. I hope you have been reassured.
Now; this concerns one George Jacob Holyoake,
H-O-L-Y, as in spirit, and O-A-K-E, tree with
an "e", a righteously English, comically English

name. One May day in 1842, this George Jacob
Holyoake, a poor young teacher, was walking
from Birmingham to Bristol to visit a friend
serving twelve months in jail for having set up
a Journal which the authorities considered to be
improper.

Mix to:

George Holyoake on the outskirts of Cheltenham.

NARRATOR: *(sound only).* His wife Madeleine was staying with
her sister in Cheltenham and Mr. Holyoake took
this opportunity to visit her on his way, but
apart from the pleasure of seeing his wife and
child again, Mr. Holyoake was in Cheltenham
for another reason. Being a member of the Social
Missionary Society and an unusually energetic
man even for an earnest time, he had arranged
to address a lecture to the local branch of the
Society.

Mix to:

Poster

NARRATOR: The subject being "Home Colonization as a
means of superseding Poor Laws and
Emigration".

Mix to:

*A kitchen—early evening. Mrs. Holyoake is
preparing soup. Mr. Holyoake is seated upon a
bench by the fire. It must be noted that Holyoake
has intense difficulty with his speech occasionally.
For example in his first line he has a considerable
obstacle to overcome in the word "pleased". This
defect must be emphasized sufficiently to appear
painful when it happens, but obviously it must be
exploited sparingly, and its later dramatic
effectiveness must depend upon the nicest discretion
of the actor and the director.*

HOLYOAKE: Your sister was not pleased to see me.

MRS. HOLYOAKE: I know.

HOLYOAKE: You seem frail, my dear.

12

MRS. HOLYOAKE: They are angry about your lecture.

HOLYOAKE: I see. Well—you are still a splendid sight for me.

MRS. HOLYOAKE: They say it is improper.

HOLYOAKE: I have missed you both.

MRS. HOLYOAKE: And further, that you are imprudent and ungracious to undertake such a thing while I am staying beneath their roof.

HOLYOAKE: Are you not giving them the twelve shillings a week I have been sending you?

MRS. HOLYOAKE: They do not think it enough.

HOLYOAKE: Not enough? A good lodging house would be cheaper but I thought you would rather be with your sister and her children.

MRS. HOLYOAKE: You are right my dear and I am grateful. George: they should have received you in the parlour.

HOLYOAKE: Cheltenham is a fashionable town and too genteel and thin for dusty boots in the parlour.

MRS. HOLYOAKE: I feel ashamed——

HOLYOAKE: Of your husband?

Mrs. Holyoake pours him his soup.

HOLYOAKE: I am sorry to see you so unhappy, Madeleine, I am indeed.

MRS. HOLYOAKE: There is some rice bread left. Will you have that?

HOLYOAKE: Thank you. I promise: you shall not stay here a day longer than necessary. I have applied for an appointment in Sheffield.

MRS. HOLYOAKE: Oh?

HOLYOAKE: To teach day school and lecture on Sundays.

MRS. HOLYOAKE: What is the salary?

HOLYOAKE: Thirty shillings a week.

MRS. HOLYOAKE: I do not mean you to think——

HOLYOAKE: The soup is good.

MRS. HOLYOAKE: To think I was ashamed of you.

HOLYOAKE: (*smiling*). It is difficult when you have relatives such as yours.

MRS. HOLYOAKE: You allow them to be insolent with you, George. They treat you like a common innkeeper.

13

HOLYOAKE: I do not earn as much as a common innkeeper.

MRS. HOLYOAKE: You seem unable to speak up for yourself.

HOLYOAKE: That is true. I do find it hard. Very hard.

MRS. HOLYOAKE: Not merely your impediment——

HOLYOAKE: No.

MRS. HOLYOAKE: But you are a man. I cannot speak for you.

HOLYOAKE: I know.

MRS. HOLYOAKE: There is more soup.

HOLYOAKE: No, thank you. I must finish preparing my lecture. We can talk about these things later.

MRS. HOLYOAKE: George, the child is poorly.

HOLYOAKE: Why, what's the matter?

MRS. HOLYOAKE: The matter is simple. She is not getting enough to eat.

HOLYOAKE: But they are being paid.

MRS. HOLYOAKE: They keep me short and there is nothing I can do. I am alone here. I tell you there is much show of things here but it is mostly pantomime. And so it is with eating and drinking.

HOLYOAKE: Surely your own sister cannot see you going short——

MRS. HOLYOAKE: They will not listen to me. They do not want to hear and it is because of you. Their dislike for you is almost past belief.

HOLYOAKE: But we have never so much as argued——

MRS. HOLYOAKE: I know it is difficult but we need you to help us, George. We need you to be strong.

HOLYOAKE: I have promised you: you will not have to remain here.

MRS. HOLYOAKE: Will you speak to them?

HOLYOAKE: I will.

MRS. HOLYOAKE: Will you speak to them now?

HOLYOAKE: Later.

MRS. HOLYOAKE: Later!

HOLYOAKE: After the lecture.

MRS. HOLYOAKE: You are avoiding it.

HOLYOAKE: I will speak to them tonight.

MRS. HOLYOAKE: No.

HOLYOAKE: I have said I will.

MRS. HOLYOAKE: No, you will not speak to them tonight, you will fasten on some evasion and that will be an end of it.

HOLYOAKE: You have my word.

MRS. HOLYOAKE: You fly from brawling like a cat from the water; yet you can speak for others well enough.

HOLYOAKE: Not well enough, not well enough. As you know.

MRS. HOLYOAKE: Oh, you are no speaker, and it's idle to pretend otherwise, (*she touches his shoulder*) but you will try your best. I am sorry.

HOLYOAKE: You are very patient.

MRS. HOLYOAKE: You will always recognize your duty and there it is. We shall all manage. (*She kisses his forehead.*) Forgive me, but you are not an easy man, and I am so anxious for the future.

HOLYOAKE: Please try to be patient. I, too, am anxious.

Mix to:

The Mechanics Hall, Cheltenham. The Chairman of the meeting, a tall, glum, middle-aged man, is speaking from the platform. Holyoake is seated beside him staring down at his hands.

NARRATOR: (*sound only*). Mrs. Holyoake was right in saying that her husband was not an impressive speaker. He was easily flustered and if, as on some occasions, he was interrupted from the floor he would usually drop his notes or even, as on one agonizing evening, dry up completely. In spite of this deficiency, he was constantly being invited to speak. He persisted and for some reason, so did his audience. Besides, there was a considerable shortage of speakers on the subject.

CHAIRMAN: I am sure you will wish to join me in offering our thanks to Mr. Holyoake for a very stimulating, provocative evening (*light applause*) and now, I think, in conclusion, we may—yes? Do you want to ask a question, sir? Another question from the floor. I think it is a little late—ah, it is Mr. Maitland. Would you mind one more question, Mr. Holyoake?

HOLYOAKE: Well——

CHAIRMAN: Very well then, just one more, Mr. Maitland, and then we really should——

MAITLAND: (*from the floor*). Sir, you have spoken at great lengths concerning our duty to man but what, sir, I would like to ask, of our duty to God?

HOLYOAKE: (*uncertainly*). Yes?

MAITLAND: Shall we not have churches and chapels in community?

HOLYOAKE: I do not wish to——

MAITLAND: That, sir, is my question.

HOLYOAKE: I do not wish to mix religion——

Voice from the floor—"Can't hear!"

HOLYOAKE: (*flustered*)—to mix religion with an economic and secular subject, but I will try to answer the question frankly.

Voice from the floor—"Hear hear!"

HOLYOAKE: Our national debt is a millstone around the poor man's neck, and our church and general religious institutions cost us about twenty million pounds annually. Worship is expensive, and so I appeal to your heads and your pockets: are we not too poor to have God? If poor men cost the state as much, they would be put, like officers, on half-pay. And while our present distress remains, it is wisest to do the same thing with Deity. (*Scattered applause.*)

MAITLAND: But, sir——

CHAIRMAN: What is it?

MAITLAND: My question has not been answered, sir.

CHAIRMAN: Come, Mr. Maitland, it is getting late.

MAITLAND: What of morality, Mr. Holyoake?

HOLYOAKE: I regard morality, but as for God, Mr. Maitland, I cannot bring myself to believe in such a thing.

CHAIRMAN: Ladies and gentlemen, it is past ten o'clock and

16

I must declare the meeting closed. Good night and thank you.

The meeting breaks up.

NARRATOR: *(sound only)*. An orderly, somewhat dull meeting came to an orderly close and the few reasonable respectable citizens of Cheltenham, who had sat the most of a spring evening on hard benches in the Mechanics Hall, walked back to their homes.

Mix to:

NARRATOR: The following day, this paragraph appeared in *The Cheltenham Chronicle*. (*He picks up a newspaper and reads from it.*) "On Tuesday evening last, a person named Holyoake, from Sheffield, delivered a lecture on Socialism, or, as it has been more appropriately termed, devilism, at the Mechanics Institute. After attacking the Church of England and religion generally for a considerable time, a teetotaller named Maitland got up and said the lecturer had been talking a good deal about our duty to man but he omitted to mention any duty towards God, and he would be glad to know if there were any chapels in the community. The Socialist then replied that he professed no religion at all and thought that they were too poor to have any. He did not believe that there was such a Being as God and impiously remarked that if there was, he would have the Deity served the same as the Government treated subalterns, by placing Him upon half pay. To their lasting shame, be it spoken, a considerable portion of the company applauded these profane opinions." At the bottom of this paragraph is a note, signed by the Editor, saying: "We have three persons in our employ who are ready to verify on oath the correctness of the above statement. We therefore hope those in authority will not suffer the matter to rest here and that some steps will be immediately taken to prevent any further publicity to such diabolical sentiments." The methods of newspaper morality have changed very little.

Mix to:

The home of Mrs. Holyoake's sister. Mrs. Holyoake, her sister and brother-in-law.

NARRATOR: *(sound only).* The next number of *The Cheltenham Chronicle* was able to announce:

BROTHER-IN-LAW: *(reading aloud).* "In reference to a paragraph which appeared in the last *Chronicle* regarding the monster, Holyoake, the magistrates read the article alluded to and expressed the opinion that it was a clear case of blasphemy. In order to check the further progress of his pernicious doctrine, the Superintendent of Police was ordered to use every exertion to bring him to justice." *(To Mrs. Holyoake.)* Read it for yourself.

Mrs. Holyoake takes newspaper and starts reading.

Mix to:

NARRATOR: By this time, Mr. Holyoake had reached Bristol, visited his friend Mr. Southwell in jail and, astonished to read the account of his meeting, set out on foot once again for Cheltenham. The evening after his arrival the owners of the Mechanics Institute, the Cheltenham Chartists, held a meeting, the subject being "Free Discussion".

Mix to:

The Mechanics Institute. The platform. Holyoake is addressing the meeting.

NARRATOR: *(sound only).* Mr. Holyoake was allowed to wind up.

HOLYOAKE: If you think it right to differ from the times and to make a stand for any valuable points of morals, do it, however rustic, however antiquated it may appear.

Mix to:

Mr. Russell, the local Police Superintendent. He
has a dozen men with him who take up positions
by the door, at the back of the little hall, and by
the gangways.

HOLYOAKE: (*sound only*). Do it not for insolence, but
seriously.

Mix to:

Russell observing the audience.

HOLYOAKE: (*sound only*) As a man who wore the soul of his
own in his bosom——

Mix to:

HOLYOAKE: ——and did not wait 'til it was breathed into him
by the breath of fashion.

(*C.U. of Holyoake struggling with the word*
"fashion".)

Mix to:

The Magistrates' Court, Cheltenham. Holyoake is
in the dock. Mr. Bubb, a local solicitor, is
speaking.

BUBB: I take my stand on the common unwritten law
of the land. There have been a variety of Statutes
based for punishing blasphemy, but these
Statutes in no way interfere with the common
unwritten law. Any person who denies the
existence or providence of God is guilty of
blasphemy and the law has an annexe to that
offence; imprisonment, corporal punishment and
fine. The offence is much aggravated by his
having put forth a placard, announcing a lecture
on a subject completely innocent and having got
together a number of persons, has given utter-
ance to these sentiments which are an insult to
God and man.

(*Mr. Bubb sits down. The Chairman of the*
Magistrates looks across at Holyoake.)

MAGISTRATE: Do you wish to add anything to the evidence you
have already given?

HOLYOAKE: I should like to remind you, sir, that in any

other town where they are better read in bigotry than Cheltenham, it is neither the custom nor the law to apprehend persons without the authority of a warrant.

MAGISTRATE: There is no justification for a warrant here.

HOLYOAKE: It is the practice for information to be laid and a regular notice to be served.

MAGISTRATE: We do not propose to argue with you. On the evidence we have heard, the case is clear. Whether you are of no religion is of little consequence to us, but your attempt to propagate the infamous sentiment that there is no God is calculated to produce disorder and confusion and is a breach of the peace. The entertaining of opinions is not opposed to law if people keep them to themselves. If they speak out of the way and seek to propagate them by undermining the institutions of the country, by denying the existence of a God, by robbing others of the hopes set before them, it is the duty of all to prevent this. And if there are any here present disposed to take up this unfortunate trade, I would assure them that as long as the law punishes and magistrates uphold the law, so long will they bring offenders to justice. So long as men say there is no God or that the religion of the state is a farce and a fallacy, these gentlemen shall not be deterred by any clamour. The prisoner will be committed to trial at the next Assizes and remanded on bail on his own recognizances of one hundred pounds and on finding two sureties of fifty pounds each.
Mix to:
The Jail, Cheltenham. Holyoake is being led into a small room where he is confronted by Captain Lefroy, the Head of the Police, and Mr. Pinching, surgeon.

LEFROY: Now, sir, this is Mr. Pinching. Would you

object to him questioning you on your opinions?

HOLYOAKE: (*hesitating*). I——

PINCHING: Mr. Holyoake: even the heathen acknowledges the existence of a Deity.

HOLYOAKE: Yes.

PINCHING: If you entertain these opinions on your death-bed, you will be a brave man, will you not?

HOLYOAKE: Death is a hard thing for any man to face. And so is life, Mr. P-p-p—— (*he stumbles on Pinching's name*).

PINCHING: The name is Pinching, sir. But you will admit, surely, that you are actuated in all this only by a love of notoriety?

HOLYOAKE: I have no relish for argument, sir, but I must defend myself.

PINCHING: Notoriety is what you relish, Mr. Holyoake, even though you seem to have a poor spirit for it.
(*To Lefroy.*) This kind is familiar enough.
(*To Holyoake.*) Do you not believe in Jesus Christ?

HOLYOAKE: This is an historical argument, sir——

PINCHING: Historical argument you say, sir, and you shall have it. You are aware that there is the same mass of evidence for the existence of Our Lord as for that of Henry V?

HOLYOAKE: My argument is not whether he lived but what he said.

PINCHING: It is Robert Owen who has made you an Atheist, is it not?

HOLYOAKE: Mr. Owen is a Socialist. I do not believe he is an Atheist.

PINCHING: Why don't you answer honestly, sir, are you an Atheist or are you not? You hesitate, don't you, Mr. Holyoake?

LEFROY: I think we should give the prisoner some respite, Mr. Pinching. From the looks of him he must have had a disturbing morning and this afternoon he must be on his way to Gloucester.

PINCHING: Your friend, Mr. Southwell, is in Bristol jail for the same offence, is he not?

HOLYOAKE: My position—— (*difficulty*)

PINCHING: Your what? Can you not speak decently like a man, sir, and in a decent manly fashion?

HOLYOAKE: My position has been rather in defence of Mr. Southwell's right to——

LEFROY: You look tired, Mr. Holyoake, I should save your breath. Jailer!

HOLYOAKE: I am not to have time to obtain bail?

LEFROY: My instruction is to commit you forthwith to Gloucester county jail.

PINCHING: Good-bye, Mr. Holyoake. Unhappily the day has gone when we might send you *and* Mr. Owen *and* Mr. Southwell to the stake.

HOLYOAKE: You may well live to see that day, Mr. Pinching.

PINCHING: I hope so, Mr. Holyoake, indeed I hope so.
Mix to:
Holyoake leaving Cheltenham on the way to Gloucester jail. He is handcuffed and accompanied by two constables.
Mix to:
The Corridor in the County Jail—Gloucester. The Governor, Captain Mason, Mr. Cooper and Mr. Jones, magistrates, are being escorted by the jailer to Holyoake's cell. They stop outside and the door is unlocked.
Mix to:
Holyoake rising:

MASON: Holyoake, these gentlemen are Mr. Cooper and Mr. Jones. If you have any questions to put to them you may do so.

HOLYOAKE: I see. You are magistrates, are you not?

COOPER: Yes. Do you wish to tender any complaint, Mr. Holyoake?

HOLYOAKE: Only that I am a prisoner.

COOPER: Nothing else?

HOLYOAKE: I have been refused the notebook and papers which I need for my defence.

JONES: The prison chaplain does not think it necessary.

HOLYOAKE: It is necessary for him that I am deprived of them. I gave him a list of the books I wanted to read for my trial and he has only allowed me thirteen of them.

COOPER: Thirteen is a large enough number surely, Mr. Holyoake.

JONES: Besides, the chaplain has told me that the other books were of an unChristian character.

HOLYOAKE: They were, sir.

JONES: So—you see?

COOPER: The chaplain tells us you have refused any spiritual consolation.

HOLYOAKE: I would like my books.

JONES: (*gently*). Do you not find this a hard course you have taken, Mr. Holyoake?

HOLYOAKE: I do, sir, I find it very hard. (*Smiling.*) It would be easier with the books.

JONES: Come now, you will be ill advised not to employ counsel.

HOLYOAKE: I shall defend myself, sir, as well as I am able.

COOPER: As well as you are able? And how well is that? Do let yourself be advised.

HOLYOAKE: I think a lawyer is not a good man to state a case of conscience.

COOPER: But able, Mr. Holyoake; how able are you?

HOLYOAKE: I shall try, sir.

COOPER: But what if you are not equipped to try. There are things some of us cannot do. What if your speech should fail you?

HOLYOAKE: I shall try, sir.

COOPER: Think on it, Holyoake. The judge will put you down and not hear you.

JONES: (*kindly*). Come, boy. You are a deist, are you not? (*Pause.*) You cannot be something else. Can you?

23

HOLYOAKE: I don't know, sir. I did not know before and I do not know now. But I do think that I am alone in this matter and will remain so.
Fade

END OF ACT ONE

ACT TWO

The Assize Court—Gloucester. Holyoake is in the dock awkwardly arranging a pile of books on the shelf in front of him. The Clerk reads the indictment as follows:

CLERK: The jurors for Our Lady the Queen, upon their oath, present that George Jacob Holyoake, late of the parish of Cheltenham, in the County of Gloucester, being a wicked and malicious and evil disposed person and disregarding the laws and religion of the realm, and wickedly and profanely devising and intending to bring Almighty God, the Holy Scriptures and the Christian religion, into disbelief and contempt among the people of this Kingdom on the twenty-fourth day of May, in the fifth year of the reign of Our Lady the Queen, with force and arms, at the parish aforesaid, in the County aforesaid, in the presence and hearing of diverse liege subjects of our said Lady the Queen, maliciously, unlawfully and wickedly did compose, speak, utter, pronounce, and publish with a loud voice, of and concerning Almighty God, the Holy Scriptures, and the Christian religion, these words following, that is to say, "I (meaning the said George Jacob Holyoake) do not believe there is such a thing as a God: I (meaning the said George Jacob Holyoake) would have the Deity served as they (meaning the Government of this Kingdom) as they serve the Subalterns, and place Him (meaning Almighty God) on half pay." To the high displeasure of Almighty God, to the great scandal and reproach of the Christian religion, in open violation of the laws of this

Kingdom, to the evil example of all others in the like case offending, and against the peace of Our Lady the Queen, her Crown and dignity.

NARRATOR: (*sound only*). Mr. Holyoake, intent on speaking in a firm, manly fashion, pleaded not guilty and applied to have the name of the jury called over singly and distinctly.
Mix to:
Mr. Alexander, Counsel for the Prosecution.

NARRATOR: (*sound only*). Mr. Alexander, Counsel for the Prosecution, said the offence only being a misdemeanour, the defendant had not right to challenge.
Mix to:
Mr. Justice Erskine.

ERSKINE: Of course not, unless reasons are given in each case.

CLERK: The name John Lovesey is first.

HOLYOAKE: I object to Lovesey. He sat on the bench when I was before the magistrates at Cheltenham and approved the proceedings against me. His is not disinterested in this matter.

ERSKINE: That is not sufficient reason for challenging.
Mix to:
Holyoake rearranging some of his books which have fallen down from his ledge into the dock.

NARRATOR: (*sound only*). The names of the jury were called over and they each took their place.
The camera follows each jury man as he takes his seat on the benches.

NARRATOR: (*sound only*). Thomas Gardiner, grocer, foreman.
James Reeve, farmer, Chedworth.
William Ellis, farmer, Chedworth.
William Matthews, poulterer, Cheltenham.
Simon Vizard, shopkeeper, Oldland.
Isaac Tombes, farmer, Whitcomb.
William Wilson, maltster, Brimpsfield.

Edwin Brown, farmer, Withington.
Bevan Smith, farmer, Harescomb.
William Smith, miller, Barnwood.
Joseph Shipp, farmer, Yate.

HOLYOAKE: Can I be allowed to read the indictment against me?

ERSKINE: Certainly.

A copy of the indictment is handed up to Holyoake.

ERSKINE: Do you require notepaper and pens?

HOLYOAKE: Thank you, sir, I do.

Mr. Alexander rises.

ALEXANDER: The defendant, on the twenty-fourth of May last, issued placards for a lecture to be delivered in Cheltenham. In this placard he announced, not the diabolical, the dreadful topics which he discanted upon, not anything which would lead the reader to imagine or to expect what really took place, but he gave out his subject as a lecture upon "Home Colonization, Emigration and the Poor Laws". Mark this, gentlemen of the jury, had he given in his announcements any hint of what was to have taken place, his end might have been defeated, and no audience attracted to listen to the blasphemous expressions you have heard set out in the indictment. But he did obtain an audience, a numerous audience, and then declared that the people were too poor to have religion. That he, himself, had no religion. That he did not believe in such a thing as a God, and—though it pains me to repeat it, that he would place the Diety upon half pay. I shall call witnesses to prove all this and then it will be for you to say if he is guilty. It may be urged to you that these things were said in answer to a question, that the innuendoes must be made out. Innuendoes! I should think it is an insult to the understandings of twelve jury men—of twelve intelligent men—to call witnesses to prove innuendoes. But I should place the case before you and leave it in your hands. I am sure I need not speak, I need not dwell upon the consequences of insulting that Deity we are as much bound as inclined to reverence. Please call James Bartram.

The name of Bartram is called. Holyoake makes notes on one of his untidy sheets of paper.
Mix to:
Bartram.

BARTRAM: I am a printer at Cheltenham, employed upon *The Cheltenham Chronicle.*

ALEXANDER: Did you attend the lecture, given by the defendant, on the twenty-fourth of May?

BARTRAM: I did, sir.

ALEXANDER: Did a placard announcing the lecture proclaim as follows, "Home Colonization, Emigration, Poor Laws Superseded."

BARTRAM: It did, sir.

ALEXANDER: At the very end of the evening was a supplementary question put to the defendant?

BARTRAM: Yes, sir.

ALEXANDER: What was that question?

BARTRAM: (*glibly*). The defendant had been speaking of our duty to man, and at the end, Mr. Maitland got up, saying he—the defendant—had said nothing of our duty toward God. At this, the prisoner said, "I am of no religion at all. I do not believe in such a thing as a God. The people of this country are too poor to have any religion. I would serve the Deity as the Government does the Subalterns—place him on half pay". He was the length of the room off, I heard him distinctly.

ALEXANDER: Thank you, Mr. Bartram.

BARTRAM: He spoke in a distinct voice.

HOLYOAKE: You say I said the people were too poor to have any religion. Will you state the reasons I gave?

BARTRAM: I think you said something about the great expense of religion to the country.

HOLYOAKE: Will you remember the other reason?

BARTRAM: I don't remember any.

HOLYOAKE: Now you have sworn the words are blasphemous——

ERSKINE: No, he has not.

HOLYOAKE: Will you state if the words are blasphemous?

ERSKINE: That question must be put through me. (*To Bartram.*) Do you consider the words blasphemous?

BARTRAM: I do.

HOLYOAKE: Why do you think them blasphemous?

BARTRAM: Because they revile the majesty of Heaven and are calculated to subvert peace, law and order. They are punishable by human law because they attack human authority.

HOLYOAKE: Who has taught you to define blasphemy in this way?

BARTRAM: I have not been taught, it is my own opinion.

HOLYOAKE: During my examination before the magistrates you did not seem to be able to express these opinions. Can you swear that you have not concocted this answer for the occasion?

BARTRAM: I was not expecting to be catechized.

HOLYOAKE: Who advised you to come here as a witness?

BARTRAM: The magistrate, sir.

HOLYOAKE: On the night you attended my lecture, did you hear me speak against morality?

BARTRAM: No, you said nothing against morality.

HOLYOAKE: What is your opinion of morality?

ERSKINE: The question is irrelevant.

HOLYOAKE: Do you think I spoke my honest convictions?

BARTRAM: I thought you spoke what you meant.

ERSKINE: You must not ask the witness to give his opinions.

HOLYOAKE: Would you have lost your situation with *The Cheltenham Chronicle* if you had not come forward in this case?

BARTRAM: No, I would not. In my opinion you spoke wickedly as stated in the indictment. You spoke of the enormous sums of money spent upon religion and the poverty of the people, and afterwards you said you would place God on half pay as the Government did Subalterns.

ALEXANDER: Mr. Bartram, how long have you been employed by *The Cheltenham Chronicle?*

BARTRAM: For ten years, sir.

ALEXANDER: Do you give evidence from fear or reward?

BARTRAM: No, sir.

ALEXANDER: You give it from a sense of duty?

BARTRAM: I do, sir.

ALEXANDER: That is the case for the prosecution, my lord.

ERSKINE: *(to Holyoake).* Now is the time for your defence.

HOLYOAKE: I am surprised to hear that the case for the prosecution is closed. I submit to Your Lordship, there is not sufficient evidence before the court,

ERSKINE: That is for the jury to decide.

HOLYOAKE: I thought, my lord, as the evidence is so manifestly insufficient to prove malice, you would have felt bound to direct my acquittal.

ERSKINE: It is for the jury to say whether they are satisfied.

HOLYOAKE: The counsel who opened the case did not state whether the indictment was as statute or common law.

ERSKINE: Common law.

HOLYOAKE: Then, gentlemen of the jury, I shall draw your attention to that, and I hope I shall be able to explain the law bearing on my case.

ERSKINE: The jury must take the law from me. I am responsible for that. If this is not an offence for common law, this indictment is worth nothing, I sit here not to correct the law but merely to administer it.

(Holyoake is flustered.)

ERSKINE: Continue.

HOLYOAKE: I—— (*he flounders.*)
ERSKINE: You must see now that you should have given your case into the hands of counsel.
HOLYOAKE: I ask you to be p-atient, my lord. It is from no disrespect to the Bar that I did not employ counsel, but because they are unable to enter into my motives. There is a magic circle of orthodoxy they will not step out of. The intention of a libel constitutes its criminality. It is for you gentlemen to say whether I knowingly, wickedly, and maliciously offended the law. Malice is necessary to a libel. Conscientious words are allowable. What, then, is my crime? For my difference in opinion with you upon the question of Deity, I offer no apology. I am under no contract to think as you do and I owe you no obligation to do so. If I asked you to give up your belief, you would think it impertinence and if you punish me for not giving up mine, how will you reconcile it with "doing as you would (*struggles*) wish to be done to"?
ALEXANDER: My lord, I find it almost impossible to hear the prisoner. Might I suggest it would help if he were to slow down his delivery.
ERSKINE: We shall wait for you, Mr. Holyoake.
HOLYOAKE: (*making more effort*). I have injured no man's reputation, taken no man's property, attacked no man's person, violated no oath, taught no immorality. I was asked a question and answered it openly. I should feel myself degraded if I descended to finding out if my convictions suited every anonymous man in the audience before I uttered them. What is the morality of a law which prohibits the free publication of an opinion?
ERSKINE: You must have heard me state the law that if it be done temperately and decently, all men are at liberty to state opinions.
HOLYOAKE: Then this liberty is a mockery. The word

31

temperate means what those in authority think proper.

ERSKINE: An honest man speaking his opinions decently is entitled to do so.

HOLYOAKE: It must be already clear enough to you, gentlemen of the jury, that I am here for having been more honest than the law happens to allow. What is this temperate? What is intemperate? Invective, sarcasm, p——

ALEXANDER: Personality.

HOLYOAKE: Thank you, Mr. Alexander.

ALEXANDER: Pleasure.

HOLYOAKE: —and the like. But these weapons are denied only to those who attack the prevailing opinion. Is it intemperate to say the Deity should be put on half pay? Did I do Him a disgrace if I thought He, who is called Our Father, the Most High, would dispose with one half of the lip service He receives from the clergy, in order to give His creatures in poverty their due?

ERSKINE: If you can convince the jury that your only meaning was that the income of the clergy ought to be reduced and that you did not intend to insult God, I should tell the jury that you ought not be convicted. You need not go into a laboured defence of that.

HOLYOAKE: I see. (*Picking up again.*) There is a strange infirmity in English minds which makes them accept a bad principle which they, as Englishmen, are no longer bad enough to put into practice. So it is with this prosecution, which is no more than the poor rags of former persecutions. In this age, as often as men introduce new benefits so do others try to bring back old evils. Gentlemen, what is this p-rosecution?
(*There is some laughter.*)

ERSKINE: We shall have no repetition of that.

HOLYOAKE: "If any of you lack wisdom," says St. James,

32

"let him ask of God but let him ask in faith."
My prosecutors have asked, and Mr. Alexander
has asked and they have put their faith in police-
men and in the common law. A good Christian
will be sure to leave the issue in God's hands.
Not the will of God but the will of bigots has
been done and the issue left in the turnkey's
hands. A short time ago, it was argued that if the
political squibs, which are seen in shop windows,
were permitted to be published, they would
bring Government into contempt. Soon you
would have no Government. Well? Their publication has been permitted. Have we no
Government now? So it is with religion. We
might challenge all the wits and caricaturists in
the world to bring the problems of Euclid into
contempt. No man can bring into contempt that
which is essential and true. Now, gentlemen, turn
to the question. What is blasphemy? It is said to
be "an injury to God". Men who could not string
six sentences together have told me they would
defend God—men I would be ashamed to have
defending me. But blasphemy is an impossibility.
What does it mean but an annoyance to God?
To believe in this is to believe in the magical
power of words and there is no magic in the
words, neither yours nor mine.
(*Holyoake is beginning to find his way and collect
himself. In the following speech he even attempts
some lightness.*)

HOLYOAKE: This blasphemy then is an antiquated accusation.
What a turmoil, what a splutter there was in this
land when men first said they would not eat fish,
that they would not bow down to priests, and
that they would not confess except when they
liked. What threats there were of Hell and flames,
what splashing about of fire and brimstone, what
judgment on these men choked with their beef

steak on a Friday. Such frying, such barbecueing and everyone dripping in a flood of sin and gravy and not the smallest notion of a red herring anyway. How fathomless must be the patience of Heaven that this island is not swallowed up in the sea for it, when we know we shall appear in the next world with so much mutton on our heads! But we have tried to look into the rules with the intelligence that has been given to us and calculated the risk that eating mutton can no longer be a blasphemy. If God be truth you libel Him and His power! It is a melancholy maxim in these courts of law that the greater the truth the greater the libel, and so it would be with me this day if I could demonstrate to you that there is no Deity. The more correct I am, the severer would be my punishment because the law regards the belief in a God to be the foundation of obedience among men. I have been told to look around the world for evidence of the truth of the Christian religion; it is easy for those who enjoy good fortune to say so. For them, everything shines brightly, but I can see cause for complaint, and I am not alone in the feeling. There are those here who think that religion can lead to general happiness; I do not, and I have had the same means of judging as yourselves. You say your feelings are insulted—your opinions are outraged; but what of mine? Gentlemen, I will not keep you much longer, but before I finish I must first give you some hint of my difficulties in this matter. What is Christian morality but the New Testament. Impressive it is, eloquent, poetic, but general and often impossible to be taken literally. You cannot eke out a whole man's morality from this. You are forced back to the Old Testament which ethic is elaborate and specific but often barbarous and intended for a

34

barbarous people. Your St. Paul rejected it, and was forced to draw on the Greeks and Romans even to the extent of sanctioning slavery. What you call your Christianity is not Christianity but your churches' work of two thousand years. I do not deny the goodness that is in it but I deny that it is more than a part of goodness. It is passive and obedient. "Thou shalt not" has precedence over "thou shalt". It has always feared the flesh and so it flees from life. It holds out hope of Heaven and the threat of Hell, indulging the fear in individual men, offering an investment instead of a contest. This is submission and I do not believe in it. Our obligation to man has come down from the Greek and the Roman. Whatever there is of personal dignity, honour, or magnanimity, comes from our human, not our religious education. You see, gentlemen, these difficulties have been insuperable for me. When I was in Cheltenham jail I was asked if I would be so brave on my death-bed. I cannot tell. My own supply of courage is hard to come by, but let me assure you that if men can expect to die in peace who can send their fellow men to jail for honest opinion, I have nothing to fear. Am I to count it a misfortune to live in modern times and among a Christian people?

ERSKINE: Gentlemen of the jury, I am not going to lay down as law that no man has a right to undertake opinions opposed to the religion of the state, nor to express them. Man is only responsible for his opinions to God, because God only can judge his motives. If men entertain sentiments opposed to the religion of the state, we require that they shall express them reverently. Christianity is ill defended by refusing audience to the objections of unbelievers, but whilst we would have freedom of inquiry restrained by no laws except those of

35

decency, we are entitled to demand on behalf of a religion which holds forth to mankind assurance of immortality, that its credit be assailed by no other weapons than those of sober discussion and legitimate reasoning. What you have to try is whether the defendant wickedly and devisedly did intend to bring the Christian religion into contempt amongst the people. You are not called upon to say whether, in your judgment, the opinions of the defendant are right or wrong, but whether he uttered these words with the intent charged in the indictment. The question is whether the words spoken were uttered with the intention of bringing God and the Christian religion into contempt. Then the charge is made out, for I tell you that it is an offence at common law. If it is not an offence, the indictment is not worth the parchment it is written on. You have to consider the language and the passage read to you from the charge of a learned judge, "it may not be going too far to state that no author or preacher is forbidden in stating his opinions sincerely. By maliciously is not meant malice against any particular individual but a mischievous intent. This is the criterion and it is a fair one. If it can be collected from the offensive levity in which the subject is treated." If the words had appeared in the course of a written paper, you would have entertained no doubt that the person who uttered these words had uttered them with levity. The only thing in his favour is that it was not a written answer. The solution given by the defendant is that although, unhappily, he has no belief in God, he had no intention of bringing religion into contempt. He went on to state that he considered it the duty of the clergymen of the establishment to have their incomes reduced by one half. If he had

36

meant this, he ought to have made use of other language. You will dismiss from your minds all statements in newspapers or other statements made out of court and consider it in reference to the evidence. If you are convinced that he uttered it with levity, with the purpose of treating with contempt the majesty of Almighty God, he is guilty of the offence. If you think he made use of these words in the heat of the argument without any such intent, you will give him the benefit of the doubt. If you are convinced that he did it with that object, you must find him guilty despite all that has been addressed to you. If you entertain a reasonable doubt of his intention, you will give him the benefit of it.

Mix to:

NARRATOR: Mr. Holyoake had finished, his voice notably stronger and his impediment astonishingly improved. He had little time to recover before the jury brought in their verdict.

Mix to:

FOREMAN: Guilty, my lord.

CLERK: And this is the verdict of you all?

FOREMAN: It is.

ERSKINE: George Jacob Holyoake, the arm of the law is not stretched out to protect the character of the Almighty. We do not assume to be the protectors of our God, but to protect the people from indecent language. Proceeding on the evidence that has been given, trusting that these words have been uttered in the heat of the moment, I shall think it sufficient to sentence you to be imprisoned in the common jail for six calendar months.

END OF ACT TWO

ACT THREE

NARRATOR: Mr. Holyoake's first trials after his committal to jail were the profusion of bells: dock bells, basin bells, jail bells, the bells of Gloucester Cathedral and prayer bells.

Mix to:

The Common Room of the jail. A large grating overhead. A few prisoners eating gruel, including Holyoake.

NARRATOR: (*sound only*). Bells and the itch. The itch being an ailment he was certain he had already caught from his fellow prisoners. More than the complaint he feared the cure. The cure being to be dipped naked into a barrel of brimstone and pitch. After this, the prisoner was left to lie for days in blankets already used by a hundred others smeared in the same way.

The heavy Cathedral bells are replaced by the prison Prayer Bell. The other prisoners get up and leave, and Holyoake is left alone with his bowl of gruel. He looks around cautiously and begins to scratch himself with rapt intensity. He is suddenly interrupted by the voice of the jailer.

JAILER: Holyoake!

(*Holyoake is startled, thinking he has been caught scratching.*)

HOLYOAKE: Yes.

JAILER: (*entry*). Holyoake!

HOLYOAKE: I am here. (*Pulling down his sleeve hastily.*)

JAILER: Did you not hear the bell?

HOLYOAKE: I did.

JAILER: All the other prisoners have gone to prayer.

HOLYOAKE: What of that?

JAILER: I can't be talked to in this way. You must go.

39

HOLYOAKE: You are wrong. I must not.

JAILER: Don't you know where you are?

HOLYOAKE: I think I am aware of it.

JAILER: Don't you know you are a prisoner?

HOLYOAKE: I am sensible of that, too.

JAILER: Well you must do as the others do and you must go to prayers.

HOLYOAKE: Then you must c- (*difficulty.*)

JAILER: What are you trying to say?

HOLYOAKE: -c-carry me.

JAILER: I'll report you to the clergyman.

HOLYOAKE: Give the clergyman my compliments and say I'll not come to prayers.

Jailer is baffled and goes out. Holyoake makes sure he is really alone again and sits down painfully to scratch.

Mix to:

C.U.—The Prison Chaplain. The Chaplain is serious, not a fool. He is merely humourless. Holyoake recognizes this immediately.

CHAPLAIN: Well, Mr. Holyoake, how is it you did not come to prayers?

HOLYOAKE: I am imprisoned on the ground that I do not believe in a God. Would you then take me to chapel to pray to one?

CHAPLAIN: If you attended the ordinances of grace it might lead you to believe.

HOLYOAKE: Then I am sorry for you, sir.

CHAPLAIN: I do not think you understand us, Holyoake, it is not you we prosecute—it is your opinions.

HOLYOAKE: Then I wish you would imprison them, sir, and not me.

CHAPLAIN: (*more an unhappy bureaucrat than an evangelist*). But you must attend prayers. It is the rule of the jail.

HOLYOAKE: I will agree to this: that when on Sundays you preach and I shall hear something new. Then I will come.

CHAPLAIN: Well, if you don't come to prayers, you shall be locked up.

HOLYOAKE: Then, sir, you must give your orders.

CHAPLAIN: Well, you will at least allow me to present you with a Bible for your private reading.

HOLYOAKE: Thank you. I shall be glad of it.

The Chaplain hands him the prison Bible.

HOLYOAKE: This is the usual prison copy, is it not?

CHAPLAIN: Yes.

HOLYOAKE: And it will figure in the next jail report to the county magistrates, will it not?

CHAPLAIN: Yes, that is the form.

Holyoake hands it back to the Chaplain.

HOLYOAKE: (*politely*). Then I should like to be presented with one worth acceptance or not at all. This book is like a dumpling. I could not endure it in my library.

CHAPLAIN: But this is the prison issue.

HOLYOAKE: The trade price is about ten pence. Surely special persons must present special needs. A thin copy bound in calf in pearl type with marginal references would be most acceptable.

CHAPLAIN: (*concerned*). An edition like that would cost half a guinea.

HOLYOAKE: Yes, sir, it is a great deal.

CHAPLAIN: We shall see. (*At the door.*) By the by, your friend, Mr. Southwell, is dead in Bristol jail.

HOLYOAKE: Southwell? When?

CHAPLAIN: Yesterday. He began to die badly and then he started to curse your name.

HOLYOAKE: That is not true.

CHAPLAIN: And he recanted at the end.

HOLYOAKE: What?

CHAPLAIN: Why, he cried out like a child and begged forgiveness of his Father. He gave himself up.

HOLYOAKE: This is a crude strategy and I am tired of them. Please leave me.

CHAPLAIN: It is the truth, Mr. Holyoake. I swear it.

(He goes out. C.U. Holyoake.)
Mix to:
Holyoake's hand, slowly, carefully scratching at his bare shoulder. The sound of footsteps and he covers himself. Mr. Jones, the magistrate, enters.

JONES: Now, how are you, sir?

HOLYOAKE: I am well, thank you.

JONES: Yes. Yes, well I suppose you are looking well enough in the circumstances. Holyoake: I seem to remember your objecting to being called a fool by me for your opinions.

HOLYOAKE: I thought it a discourtesy, yes, sir.

JONES: I also remember you speaking with a surprising respect for some of the German theologians.

HOLYOAKE: Yes.

JONES: It might interest you to know that one of them has just published a new translation of the Psalms of David. I have brought it with me as a matter of fact. Now see there: the fourteenth psalm, "The fool hath said in his heart: there is no God."

Holyoake stares back at Mr. Jones.

JONES: *(gently)*. You see, Mr. Holyoake, David says you are a fool.

Holyoake looks at him with some affection.

HOLYOAKE: I do not respect rudeness in the mouth of David any more than in yours, Mr. Jones. *(He scratches surreptitiously.)*

JONES: *(glad of the diversion)*. Do you scratch, sir?

HOLYOAKE: No, sir. It is an old nervous impediment like my speech. Mr. Jones, will you be so good as to tell me the truth about my friend Mr. Southwell, in Bristol jail?

JONES: What have you heard?

HOLYOAKE: That he recanted on his death-bed.

JONES: It is true.

(Mr. Jones rises, troubled.)

JONES: I ask you to forgive me, Mr. Holyoake, I have

42

conducted this interview very clumsily indeed
and I am very sorry.

HOLYOAKE: Well?

JONES: Letters have come to the Governor's hands
concerning your daughter.

HOLYOAKE: My daughter? Is she sick?

JONES: She is. To dying. If not already dead. I thought
you would prefer me to tell you.

HOLYOAKE: Thank you.

JONES: I shall arrange for Mrs. Holyoake to come and
see you as soon as she is able. You shall have the
use of the Magistrates' Committee Room. It is a
furnished cheerful apartment.

HOLYOAKE: Thank you.

JONES: Yes. Mr. Holyoake? (*Tentatively.*) Would you
permit me to say a prayer?
(*Holyoake turns back to him.*)

HOLYOAKE: If it pleases you, Mr. Jones, if it pleases you.
(*Mr. Jones kneels while Holyoake stands beneath
the cell window. The two figures are silhouetted.*)

JONES: O Almighty God with Whom do live the spirits
of just men made perfect, if they are delivered
from their earthly prisons; we humbly commend
the soul of this Thy servant, our dear sister, into
thy hands, as into the hand of a faithful Creator
and most merciful Saviour; most humbly beseech-
ing Thee that it may be precious in Thy sight.
Mix to:
*C.U. Mrs. Holyoake, Magistrates' Committee
Room.*

MRS. HOLYOAKE: We made the arrangements for the burial at the
Birmingham cemetery. The clerk asked whether
we would provide a minister or whether friends
of the deceased would do so, so I told him a
minister was not desired.
The camera tracks back to take in Holyoake.

MRS. HOLYOAKE: Then the clerk said, "You mean you will provide
one yourself?" so I said again we did not require

43

one at all. Please send the beadle only. And on the day of the interment, the beadle came as you instructed. We did everything as you instructed. We told him to conduct the burial party direct to the grave and not into the chapel, and he did it without a word. The coffin was plain but very pretty, without tinsel or angels, and we all threw in a bouquet of flowers as it was lowered in. And when the grave was made up, we went home. She was buried without parade, without priest, or priestly ceremony. It was just as you instructed. (*Pause.*) You may have your opinions, George, but I know now: this was not a manly thing to have done and I can't thank you for it. No not that even. I cannot ever forgive you for it.

HOLYOAKE: I would rather regret my fortune—than—than be ashamed of my v-victory.

MRS. HOLYOAKE: There is no victory in this, George, and your future—you will regret that for the rest of your life. (*She rises.*) Except for two, none of your colleagues have sent a friendly word.

HOLYOAKE: What about Mr. Owen?

MRS. HOLYOAKE: Mr. Robert Owen. What a debt we owe to him! He has not recognized your existence, even by a single line. When you leave this place you will walk over the grave of your own child. Well? Where is your tongue now, Mr. Holyoake? (*C.U. of Mrs. Holyoake.*)
Mix to:
The Prison Chapel. The Chaplain walks down the aisle, followed by Holyoake. He motions him into one of the spiked prisoners' pews and ascends into the pulpit. The Chaplain prays while Holyoake stands staring ahead of him.

CHAPLAIN: Hear my prayer, O Lord, and let my cry come unto Thee. Hide not thy face from me in the time of my trouble: incline thine ear unto me

44

when I call: O hear me and that right soon. For
my days are consumed away like smoke and my
bones are burnt up as it were a fire brand. My
heart is smitten down and withered like grass: so
that I forgot to eat my bread. For the voice of
my groaning: my bones will scarce cleave to my
flesh. I am become like a pelican in the wilderness
and like an owl that is in the desert. I have
watched and am even as it were a sparrow that
sitteth alone upon the house top and that because
of thine indignation and wrath for Thou hast
taken me up and cast me down. My days are
gone like a shadow and I am withered like grass.
Do you not see what you have done? Can you
not speak? But Thou, O Lord, shalt endure
for ever and Thy remembrance throughout all
generations. Holyoake, where are you?
C.U. Holyoake.

CHAPLAIN: O Blessed Lord, the Father of mercies, and the
God of all comforts; we beseech thee, look down
in pity and compassion upon this thy afflicted
servant. Thou writest bitter things against him,
and makest him to possess his former iniquities;
thy wrath lieth hard upon him, and his soul is
full of trouble: but, O merciful God, who hast
written Thy holy Word for our learning, that
we, through patience and comfort of thy holy
Scriptures, might have hope; give him a right
understanding of himself and of thy threats and
promises; that he may neither cast away his
confidence in thee, nor place it anywhere but in
thee. Give him strength against all his tempta-
tions, and heal all his distempers. Break not the
bruised reed, nor quench the smoking flax. Shut
not up thy tender mercies in displeasure; but
make him to hear of joy and gladness, that the
bones which thou hast broken may rejoice.
Deliver him from fear of the enemy, and lift up

45

the light of Thy Countenance upon him, and
give him peace, through the merits and medita-
tion of Jesus Christ our Lord. Amen. Do you
see what you are and what you have done?
Speak, Holyoake, why do you not speak?
(*C.U. Holyoake makes an animal effort to speak
but nothing will happen.*)
Mix to:
*The courtyard, early morning. Inside the prison,
Holyoake is being escorted to the reception gates.
Captain Mason, the Governor, is waiting for him.*

MASON: Good-bye, Holyoake.
(*Holyoake nods.*)
MASON: Good-bye and God bless you.
HOLYOAKE: (*presently*). Good-bye. It has been a rare
p-rivilege.
(*They look at each other and Mason begins to
laugh, in an uncontrolled, ironic sympathy.
Holyoake smiles back at him. The outer gates open
and he walks through into the cold December early
morning as Mason's laughter follows him.
Mix to:*)
NARRATOR: This is a time when people demand from enter-
tainments what they call a "solution". They
expect to have their little solution rattling away
down there in the centre of the play like a motto
in a Christmas cracker.
(*He starts folding up a manuscript, and puts it into
a briefcase.*)
NARRATOR: For those who seek information, it has been
put before you. If it is meaning you are looking
for, then you must start collecting for yourself.
And what would you say is the moral then?
(*He picks up the case and starts to go.*)
NARRATOR: If you are waiting for the commercial, it is
probably this: you cannot live by bread alone.
You must have jam—even if it is mixed with
another man's blood.

46

(The door opens and a policeman's feet appear.)

NARRATOR: That's all. You may retire now. And if a mini-car
is your particular mini-dream, then dream it.
When your turn comes you will be called.
Good night.
*(He walks out. The camera follows him and pans
up to a close-up of the policeman standing
at the door. The Narrator walks deliberately down
the prison corridor to his client.)*

THE END